FRIENDS

Written by
Theron Parker

Illustrated by
Daniel Winship

© 2015 by Theron Parker

ISBN 978-0-9863552-2-6

Printed in the United States of America

This book is dedicated to my boys, Elon and Nash.

Do you know how to fingerspell the alphabet?

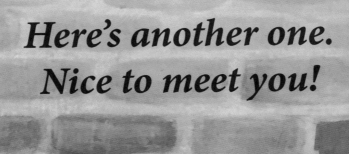

Nice to meet you.

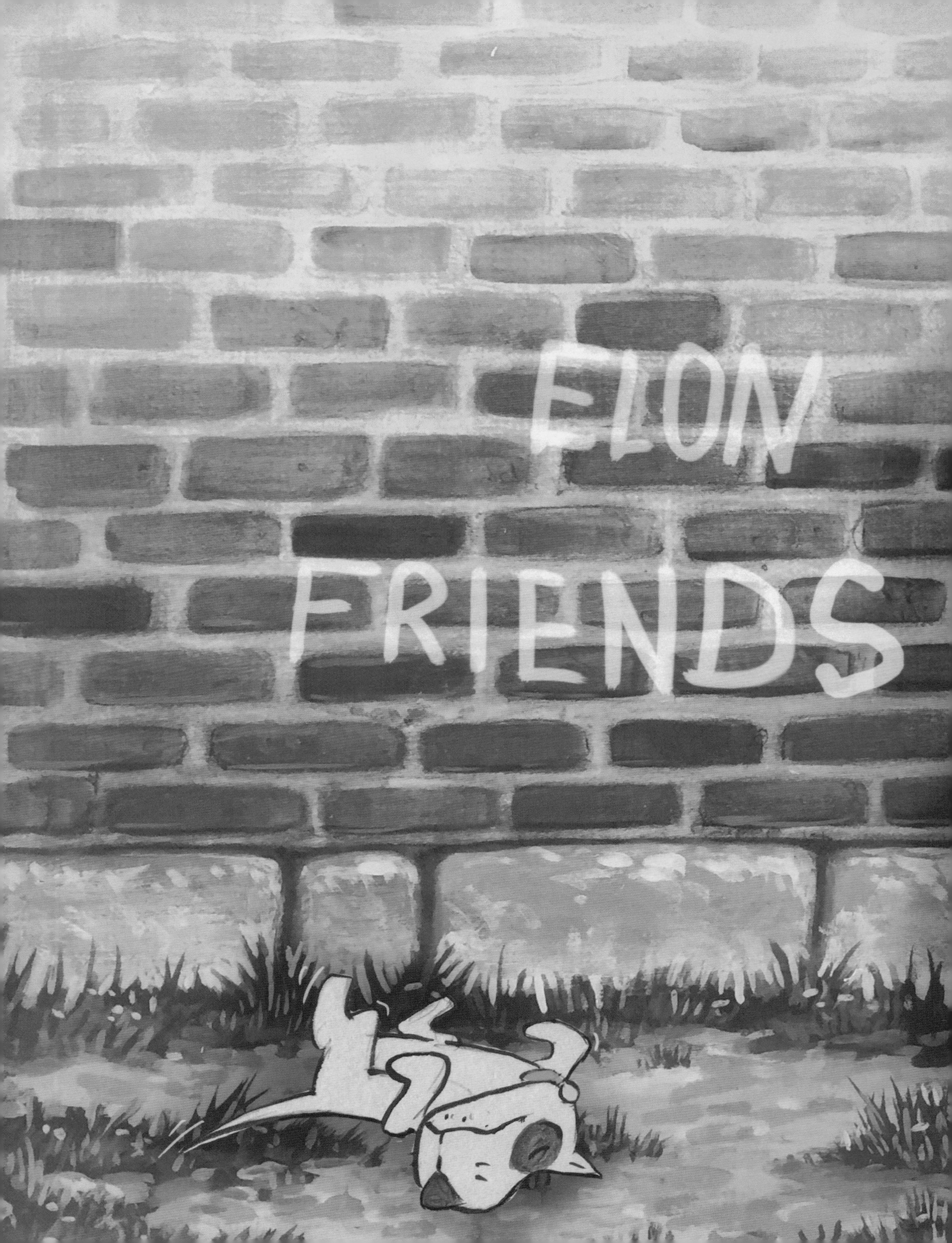
ELON
FRIENDS

About Theron Parker

Theron Parker leads a notable career as a performer, instructor and presenter. Renowned for his ABC stories, Theron has produced four DVDs: *In the Minds of Ed and Theron, Have ASL, Will Travel: Fables from Around the World, Folklore from Around the World,* and *Little Deaf Spies*. Theron also appeared in *Forget Me Not*, and served as an assistant producer for ASL Films. A certified Baby Signs instructor, he teaches literacy through American Sign Language for his non-profit organization, ABC ASL, and through his videos on YouTube. For Theron, ASL storytelling is the most beautiful music imaginable. He aspires to expose as many deaf children and hearing people as possible to the natural beauty and expressiveness of ASL. With several books in the works, Theron wishes to thank his partner Mindy Moore for igniting the spark that led to this book.

About Daniel Winship

Daniel Winship is a Deaf artist who was born and raised in Maine. With a bachelor's degree in illustration from the Ringling College of Art and Design, Daniel works in illustration among other medias, and is thrilled to be part of this book. He lives in Maine with his family, and together, they enjoy the seasons and activities Maine offers, including hiking, cross-country skiing, and biking.

Made in the USA
Lexington, KY
04 January 2016